Young Lions

The Witch on Holiday

The witch often thought how clever she was. It was just a pity that very few other people agreed with her. In fact, they rarely noticed her except to say, "Don't go too near that old lady, she looks a bit . . . er . . . peculiar." And that sort of thing.

"Do you notice me?" she asked Simon suddenly.

"Of course I do!" laughed Simon.

"Oh well," muttered the witch, "you're used to me – I nearly frightened your mother to death and she still didn't notice me much."

"Well," said Simon, "that's probably because you don't go out much or do anything special."

"I'm going to join the Fire Service," the witch told him. "I'm good at putting out fires. I'm going to be a firewoman. That's fairly special."

"A firewoman!" said Simon. "They don't have women in the Fire Service."

"Not yet they don't," said the witch . . .

Also by Margaret Stuart Barry

Simon and the Witch
The Return of the Witch
The Witch of Monopoly Manor
The Witch V.I.P.
Simon and the Witch in School
The Witch and the Holiday Club

Margaret Stuart Barry

The Witch
on Holiday

Illustrated by Linda Birch

Young Lions
An Imprint of HarperCollinsPublishers

First published by
William Collins Sons & Co Ltd 1983
First published in Young Lions 1984
Ninth impression July 1992

Young Lions is an imprint of
HarperCollins Children's Books, a division of
HarperCollins Publishers Ltd,
77–85 Fulham Palace Road, Hammersmith,
London W6 8JB

ISBN 0 00 672300-4

Printed and bound in Great Britain by
HarperCollins Manufacturing, Glasgow

Contents

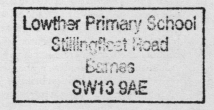

To my Mother

The Boring Camping Holiday

The witch was busy polishing the star, which shone above her cooker, when Simon arrived. Simon had come to visit the witch because she was one of his very best friends. He hadn't seen her for a while and was afraid she might have gone away.

"No I haven't," said the witch, putting the star back cock-eyed on the wall. "Do you think I'm *made* of holidays?"

Simon looked puzzled. The witch didn't go to work, and she didn't have to go to school, except when she was in the mood, so he reckoned she was on holiday all the time.

"Hah!" snapped the witch, "there's a difference. *Being* on holiday, and *going* on one, are two entirely different things."

Simon looked even more puzzled and was afraid to say that that was what he'd come round to tell her, that he was *going* on a holiday.

"Hah again!" snorted the witch. "Children these days are very spoilt. They go to school for a few weeks, and they do a few easy sums, and they read a few easy books, and they spell a few easy words, and they draw a few easy pictures, and they sing a few easy songs, and they play a few easy games, and they stand on a few easy heads, and then they think they have to go on a holiday."

Just then, George, who was the witch's cat, prowled in. If ever an animal needed a holiday, here was one who did. George was thin and scrawny and his black fur stuck up in dusty tufts. He had one green eye and one yellow eye, both of which rolled in different directions.Sometimes, the yellow eye would turn red and sometimes the green eye would turn orange – like a set of traffic lights. George didn't hunt for mice, the way most cats do, he hunted for furniture and ate it. There was hardly a chair in the witch's house which did not collapse when you sat on it. He began to chew at one of the legs of the television which he shouldn't have done because it was only rented.

But the witch ignored him and said to Simon, "Well, this holiday you're going on, where are you going on it to?"

"It's a camping holiday," said Simon. "I'm going with the school."

The witch had never heard of "camping" and she ran into the sitting room while Simon wasn't looking and looked up her Book Of Magic Spells. But all she could find under the letter 'C' was C for Custard, C for Catastrophe, and C for Christmas.

"Will there be any custard catastrophes on this trip?" she asked, slyly.

"No," said Simon.

"Or sledges and snow, and such like?" asked the witch.

"I hope not!" said Simon. "It's summertime."

"Oh," said the witch, pretending not to look surprised.

But as soon as Simon had gone, she decided to follow him on his camping holiday and find out what it was all about.

The witch *did* know that it was polite to pack a toothbrush and a face flannel so she magicked them up with her wand. She also stuffed into her case some beetle and spider sandwiches, her Magic Spell book, and her cat, George, just in case he should gobble up 'Coronation Street' while she was away.

A large group of children was standing at the

bus stop waiting for a special bus. The witch was amazed to see that the children were covered all over with luggage. Each child had a big waterproof lump on its back, out of which stuck sticks and other weird objects.

"Camping looks heavy. And bristly!" thought the witch.

Simon himself looked like a small hedgehog.

Not so small, but just as bristly was a man the witch didn't like much. He was Mr Bodley, the headmaster. He was a man who couldn't take a joke, and he boomed a lot.

The bus came and the hedgehogs climbed on. The witch, not wishing to be discovered so early

on the holiday, tied herself with string to the back bumper of the coach and fell asleep. When she awoke, there were bumpy hills all around her and lots of Christmas trees and a lake. There were no supermarkets or cars or funfairs.

"Perhaps we've just broken down in the middle of nowhere," thought the witch.

But the children were getting off the coach. In apple-pie order, they marched over a little bridge, round the side of the lake, and then stopped in a large field. The witch followed them, slithering somewhat unnecessarily like a long black snake through the hedges.

"They've stopped," she muttered to George,

who was still fastened up inside the suitcase and couldn't hear her. "I wonder if they've broken down like the coach?"

But the children were beginning to put up tents.

The witch could remember going to a circus once where there'd been a big cloth house, held up with poles. These cloth houses were much smaller and rather silly.

"Is *this* the 'camping' thing then?" the witch asked Simon, flopping out of the hedge like a large black umbrella which had seen better days.

"Hey!" gasped Simon, alarmed. "*You* shouldn't be here! How did you get here?"

"Same as you did; on the bus. Tied on with string," said the witch.

"Hey!" said Mr Bodley, the Head — aghast at the sight of the witch, who, in the past, had turned the school gardener into a frog, wrecked his office, and caused havoc at the school pantomime.

"*You* shouldn't be here! How did you get here?"

"I came on Concorde!" snapped the witch. "I've come on a camping holiday."

"Oh no, you haven't!" said Mr Bodley, noticing, wickedly, that the witch had no tent. "There's no room." And he walked away.

The witch followed Simon up and down the field, watching him unpack, and prop up his little cloth house with poles, and pegs and ropes.

"Now!" said the witch, squeezing in after Simon. But there was no room for her, not even when she took off her hat.

"It's no good," puffed Simon. "I'd *like* you to stay but I'm afraid you'll just have to go home."

The witch had no intention of going home, and unpacked her toothbrush and her cat. George, who had been imprisoned and forgotten for six hours, shot out of the case and hungrily devoured the poles which were to have propped up Mr Bodley's tent. Luckily, Mr Bodley had wellingtoned off to the brook for a kettle of water, so didn't see him.

At that moment, Simon's school friends noticed the witch. "Eeeee!" they squealed, half delighted and half scared. "*You* shouldn't be here!"

"Listen!" said the witch, sticking her nose at them and twitching the spot on the end of it. "If you lazy, yelling lot of little lay-abouts need a camping holiday, then so do I."

Jimmy Watson shivered in his training shoes. But Sally, (who was now the best reader in the class – if not in the whole world) said, "Huh!"

Just then, Miss Phoeble, the form mistress,

arrived. "Come along girls," she said.

The witch sprang to the front of the queue.

Miss Phoeble, who had tried to give in her notice lots of times but couldn't find another school which would take her, gave a little scream.

"*You're* not a girl!" she started to say and then changed it into, "You don't appear to have a tent."

"Pah!" snorted the witch, now really annoyed. "All this talk about tents."

And she flung herself furiously into the middle of her Book Of Magic Spells and found T for Tornado, T for 2 times 2, and T for Try . . .M.

Under M was the word Marquee – which means Very Large Tent. So the witch whipped her wand in the air and the most enormous tent started to blow itself up. It went on blowing itself up until it was so big it made the rest of the tents look like pocket handkerchiefs.

"Goodnight," said the witch, flouncing into the marquee with a swish of her face flannel and a jab in the air with her toothbrush.

"Gosh!" said Jimmy Watson, grinning in terror and delight.

"*More* show-offing!" snorted Sally.

Next morning, everyone was up bright and early, frying sausages. The witch was even more puzzled. Cooking was housework. Was housework a holiday? Probably something more exciting was going to happen soon.

The children plodded off to the stream to wash their dishes.

"Well, a little later on," mumbled the witch.

The children went for a ramble and looked at flowers, and stones, and sticklebacks.

"Perhaps tonight then," thought the witch. "Probably there'll be a firework display, or an egg and spoon race, or a game of Cowboys and Indians with Mr Bodley as Big Chief Nasty chasing Miss Phoeble playing Minny Moan-a-Lot."

But no such games took place. Instead, the children sat tidily round the camp fire and sang songs.

The witch was *enormously* disgusted. She had only been on one or two holidays in the whole of her life but this was definitely the rottenest. It was the headmaster's fault, she decided. He didn't know how to make a children's holiday exciting enough.

She flumped away into the darkness and sat under a hedge. A warm smell wafted towards her and the sound of heavy breathing. The witch found herself looking eyeball to eyeball at a large brown and white monster. It had a big wet nose and horns. Behind it were ninety-nine other monsters, all similar. They blinked their blonde eyelashes and stared at the witch. One of them swished its tail and the witch guessed it was anxious to do battle.

"How splendid!" she thought, and herded the hundred horned beasts back to the camp. Unfortunately, everyone had gone to bed. Never mind, they could play poking noses into tents. The monsters just felt in the mood for doing that anyway and started to do it at once. At first they did it sleepily, but as they grew more curious they pushed their noses further and further into the tents and swayed their heads about – mooing.

The biggest monster noticed that Miss Phoeble had an apple by her pillow and hoofed heavily towards it. It scrunched the apple loudly in Miss Phoeble's ear and she woke up screaming, "A cow!"

She was more terrified of cows than of burglars and earthquakes, and flew out of the tent faster than the speed of sound – only to find that there was a whole herd of cows stamping around. They were trampling on the guy ropes, chewing at the tent flaps, and anything else they could find which looked unusual. The children were in fits

of laughter. It made searching for sticklebacks and singing camp songs seem silly. And the cows looked so funny; all mooing and chewing. But Mr Bodley didn't think so. He bellowed like a mad bull.

Unfortunately, the cows didn't know that Mr Bodley was a teacher, let alone a headmaster, so they ignored him. Everyone had to wait patiently until the cows got fed up and went away. But by that time, the only place left for the campers to spend the rest of the night was in the witch's marquee.

"I bet you're glad I came," beamed the witch.

Mr Bodley went purple but couldn't trust himself to say anything. Next day, he packed up what was left of the camp and took the children straight home. He was strangely quiet, and Miss Phoeble shrank on a back seat, looking pale and sick. But the children chattered and giggled. They thought Simon's friend was a nuisance most of the time but this summer she had really livened up their holiday.

"I'm afraid Mr Bodley will never let you come into our school again," said Simon.

"That doesn't matter," said the witch. "I don't like the sums you're doing at the moment anyway. I'll come when you start something more interesting."

George and the Other Cat

The witch had had enough of headmasters and children and boring old cows on camping holidays and decided to go and visit some of her relatives. She looked up her address book. There was Winnie from Wapping, Hatty the Howl, Gertie the Great, Overbearing Bertha, and many others. She had stayed with all of those not so long ago. There was of course her sister, Tombola. But she lived in Africa and that was a bit out of the way.

Who else? Her finger ran down the long list of witches to whom she was related until it came to the name of Sarah Screech.

"Goodness!" said the witch, "I haven't seen Sarah for at least a hundred years."

To the witch's surprise, Sarah Screech was in the phone book.

"She must be quite posh," said the witch to George. "Go and wash your filthy whiskers."

George slunk sulkily up to the bathroom, scowled at himself in the mirror, and slunk down again.

It was dark, and the last bus had gone, so the witch got out her broomstick. A few hours later she arrived at Sarah Screech's house. She was a bit annoyed to see that it was about ten times bigger than her own little old house and much cleaner looking. Also, it was not joined to lots of other houses but stood on its own in a spacious garden. A goldfish pond glinted in the moonlight and neat roses were asleep round the doorway. The witch combed her straggling hair with her fingers and rang the bell.

Sarah Screech was a tall, thin witch. She was dressed from head to foot in shiny, black satin and wore lovely beads which swung down to her ankles.

"I'm one of your relatives," announced the witch.

Sarah Screech looked at the fat lady who was standing on her doorstep; at the remains of half a beetle sandwich stuck to her dress; the hat tied with a shoelace to her collar, and the black woolly stockings which hung like concertinas over the top of her shoes.

"I'm not sure I recollect," shuddered Sarah.

"*You* know. . ." the witch went on, "related to Winnie from Wapping, Hatty the Howl, Gertie the Great, Overbearing Bertha, sister of Tombola of Africa. Related also to Dr Livingstone, cousin to the Queen of England, thirteen times removed." (Removed by force from the gate of Buckingham Palace for disorderly behaviour).

Instantly, on mention of the Queen, Sarah screeched, "Well, how lovely to see you!"

George tried to escape into the bushes but the witch grabbed him by the tail and followed Sarah into the house.

As soon as the witch saw how splendid it was, she was sorry she'd come. Everything was covered in cream velvet. Even the carpet was cream, which the witch thought was stupid as her footprints immediately showed up on it. There were as many flowers inside the house as there were outside. But worst of all, there were two, large, cream-coloured cats. Two!

The witch tried to hide her own scruffy-looking George by half sitting on him, but Sarah Screech had already noticed George quite a lot, as his black dusty hairs had stuck themselves to nearly everything in the room. The witch was glad when it was bedtime. But even in bed she felt cross. The sheets were not only white, they were dead clean too. She fell asleep at once. But, as usual, she had forgotten to feed her cat. So, again as usual, George had to look around for something wooden to eat. At four o'clock in the morning he had finished eating the bed legs and the witch collapsed onto the floor.

"It's time we were leaving anyway," she remarked, kicking George smartly.

Remembering she had wonderful good manners she wrote a note for Sarah Screech.

S'bean luvly to see yoo
Yor bed's got wudwurm
Must fly.

And she flew off on her broomstick.

The witch was glad to be back in her own small house with the tiny front garden full of cabbages, and nasturtiums which straggled over the wall and half way up the bus stop. But she could not help thinking that Sarah Screech had *two* cats whereas she herself only had one.

"That's easy," said Simon. "Just get another."

"The police would catch me!" snapped the witch.

"I don't mean steal one," laughed Simon. "I mean buy one from the pet shop."

The witch hadn't known that one actually *bought* cats, but she set off at once to the pet shop.

"Here comes a nice old granny," thought the pet shop man, and tried to sell her a budgie, and then a mouse, and then a tortoise, and then an angel fish.

"I want that white cat," said the witch.

"Ah, you mean Plumpkin."

"Will it stay clean?" asked the witch.

"Well of course she will," said the pet shop man, not knowing the witch's house.

The witch took Plumpkin home and sat her on the hearthrug.

When George came home, his eyes bulged with disbelief. There was a fat white cat sitting on his hearthrug. A *clean* white cat, purring away like a motor bike. And when Plumpkin saw George – looking like a torn lump of matting the bin men had left behind, she shuddered, and spread herself out to make quite sure there was no room for George whom she considered to be exceedingly common.

The witch gave Plumpkin a whole tin of Pussy's Delight and hurried off to play bingo. She forgot about George's tea.

Plumpkin preened and spread herself out even more fatly across the hearthrug. She didn't want the scruffy black cat anywhere near her. George's fur stuck up in angry black tufts. As soon as Plumpkin had gone out into the yard for a moment, he scratched great big holes in the hearthrug. Plumpkin would definitely get the blame for that. But when the witch came back from bingo, cross because she hadn't won, she slapped George for ruining the rug and gave

Plumpkin a cushion to sit on.

Plumpkin narrowed her yellow eyes and purred like *two* motor bikes.

Next day, George put a rubber mouse into Plumpkin's milk which nearly choked her, but the vet got the mouse out again and ticked the witch off for being cruel. George pretended he'd never heard of rubber mice, but he got slapped again.

Meanwhile, the witch invited Hatty the Howl and Winnie from Wapping to tea – just to show off to them that she too had two cats.

"She's beautiful!" said Winnie, green with envy.

"Why don't you get rid of George now?" howled Hatty. "He's no credit to you, dear."

George was flabbergasted and Plumpkin roared like ten motor bikes in a Grand Prix. She now had a smart collar round her neck with a little bell on it.

George would have liked to hang a ten-ton church bell around her neck. He thought the witch had gone bananas. If the tiniest speck landed on Plumpkin, she'd Hoover her. And then George had a brilliant idea: all he had to do was to get the stupid cat *really* dirty. He collected some soot from the chimney and sprinkled it over Plumpkin whilst she was snoozing. But the witch shampooed the white cat and hung her on the washing line to dry.

"Soot comes off too easily," thought George, darkly. And then he had one of his specially brilliant ideas. There were some men laying tar in the High Street. He brushed himself affection-ately against Plumpkin and tried to make both his green eye and his red eye look kind. Then he fetched her a real mouse to eat and poured her the top of the cream off the milk. Plumpkin, who was not very bright, looked impressed. When George suggested they should now go for a nice little walk, she followed him. He led her through the streets, stopping her with his paw at each kerb and making her look carefully each way. Plumpkin was even more impresed. George was a horrible-looking cat, but he was obviously quite good hearted, thought Plumpkin.

Then they came to the High Street and the glistening black tar shone in the sunlight. George waved his paw politely and told the white cat, please to go first. Immediately, Plumpkin was stuck by all four paws in the wet tar. At once, she knew she'd been tricked by this nasty black cat, and struggled violently. She got her paws unstuck but fell on her back. She wriggled and rolled around in the tar until every single bit of her was black. She was even blacker than George and a lot messier.

One of the workmen said, "Gosh! there's a messy looking moggy ruining me road!" and dumped her on the pavement.

It was a slow walk home. Slow, because Plumpkin's paws had lost their prowl. It was windy too, and anything that was blowing around stuck itself to her fur. Things like leaves and bus tickets and potato crisp bags. By the time they got back, Plumpkin was a hideous sight.

"Sufferin' cats!" exclaimed the witch. "What is it?"

George smiled behind his paw and made one eye look worried and the other one puzzled. He helpfully pulled a few bus tickets off the cat to show that it was Plumpkin. The witch was

furious, and still furious when Simon came.

"I think my mother knows how to get tar off things," he said.

"Well, she can get the tar off that thing! And she can keep it," shrieked the witch, handing over Plumpkin in disgust. She'd been spending half her pension money feeding the wretched cat anyway.

George, still smirking, yawned vastly, stretched himself out to about three times his own length, and then curled up on the torn hearthrug.

Simon took poor Plumpkin home, and in a short time, Simon's mother had her cleaned up and comfortable again.

The Firewoman

One day not long after that, the torn hearthrug went on fire and the witch put it out with a bottle of lemonade. There was a lot of smoke everywhere and soot on the furniture but the witch thought, "That was clever of me! Anyone else would have called the fire brigade."

The witch often thought how clever she was. It was just a pity that very few other people agreed with her. In fact, they rarely noticed her except to say, "Aaah, poor thing!" or, "Don't go too near that old lady, she looks a bit . . . er . . . peculiar." And that sort of thing.

The witch went round to see Simon and surprised him by appearing suddenly at the kitchen window and saying, "Do you notice me?"

"Of course I do!" laughed Simon.

"Oh well," muttered the witch, "you're used to me."

She tried Simon's mother who was making the beds.

"Do you notice me?" she asked, zooming out from under the bed.

"Wowch!" exclaimed Simon's mother. "You nearly frightened me to death! Simon's downstairs."

"I nearly killed your mother," said the witch, grinning, "but she still didn't notice me all that much."

"Well," said Simon, "that's probably because she doesn't really believe you're a real witch — and you don't go out much or do anything special."

"I'm going to join the Fire Service," the witch told him. "I'm good at putting out fires. I'm going to be a firewoman. That's fairly special."

"A firewoman!" said Simon. "They don't have women in the Fire Service."

"Not yet they don't," said the witch.

When she arrived at the fire station, the men were playing cricket in the yard. They were playing cricket because no one's house was on fire.

"I've come for a job," announced the witch.

"We've got a cleaner already," said Harry, who was batting.

"I want some wellies, and a yellow mac and a tin hat."

"Run along home, Gran," said Bill, who was bowling.

"And a hosepipe," continued the witch.

The Chief Fire Officer came out and said, "We don't have women in the Fire Service."

"Women are allowed to be in anything they like," said the witch. "It said so in the paper."

The Chief Fire Officer had read the same newspaper and he was frightened that the mayor, with whom he wanted to stay friends, would be cross with him if he broke the law, so he provided the witch with a uniform.

"Thank you," said the witch, pulling on her new wellies, a mac, and a helmet, and storing her pointed hat in a locker. "So when's the next fire then?"

"Next year, I hope," said Bill, who was bowling.

But the witch thought that was very boring, so she craftily searched in her handbag for her magic wand and set Harry's bat on fire.

"Blimey!" yelled Harry, as the ball shot straight through his burnt bat. "What on earth's 'appening?"

The witch quickly squirted him out with a hosepipe.

"Did you notice me doing that?" she asked the Chief Fire Officer.

"It happened a bit too fast," said the Chief Fire Officer, stonily. "Ladder practice!"

He thought the old woman would be too stiff to get up and down the ladder, but the witch was up it and down again before the others had even finished their game of cricket.

"Squirting practice!" bawled the Chief Fire Officer.

And the witch had watered all the flowers and made a lake big enough to start a yachting race on

before Harry and Bill had finished putting on their waterproofs.

"My socks is soaking!" complained Harry.

He was still moaning about his socks when the witch leapt into the fire engine and drove off.

It was lovely driving the red fire engine. It made a great deal of noise. Cars and lorries automatically slowed down to let the witch pass.

"People take a lot of notice of a fire engine," thought the witch, pleased.

She stopped at her own house to see if her hearthrug was properly out. But unfortunately, she had poured so much lemonade on it, it was not worth undoing the fire hose.

As it happened, there was a meeting going on at the Town Hall. The Town Hall was a very large building and very important people went in it. The witch stopped the fire engine in front of a NO PARKING sign and peered through one of the windows. Round a table sat the vicar, Lady Fox-Custard, and the mayor. They were talking about a new supermarket which was going to be built on the edge of the town.

"Splendid idea," the vicar was saying. "I'll not have to travel so far for m'beans." (Beans on toast was the only meal the vicar knew how to cook.)

"Nonsense!" Lady Fox-Custard was saying. "A nasty new supermarket will spoil my view of the buttercup meadow. Let the people have it somewhere else."

The mayor, who wanted to stay friends with the vicar and Lady Fox-Custard, looked worried and lit a cigar. A thin curl of smoke wiggled up into the air and wrapped itself round the ancient beams of the ceiling.

"Hah!" thought the witch. "Smoke!"

She demolished the window with her axe, and charging in with her hosepipe, she squirted the mayor's cigar out.

"Hey!" said the mayor. "What do you think you're doing?"

"I thought you were on fire," said the witch.

"She thought no such thing," snorted Lady Fox-Custard. "She's nothing but a trouble-maker. I know that wretched woman. She's an old witch!"

"Hush," said the vicar, shocked. "I'm sure the good woman was just trying to do her job."

"Her *job!*" screeched Lady Fox-Custard. "Whoever heard of a woman being a fireman?"

"Firewoman," said the witch.

"I'm afraid it's the new law," said the mayor, soggily, squeezing water out of the fur on his robes.

"S'new law," repeated the witch, giving the stuck up Foxy-Custard a smug smirk.

Back at the station, the men were still playing cricket because they had no fire engine. When the witch returned, making as much lovely noise as she possibly could with the klaxon horns, the Chief Fire Officer said, "I know you're new here, but you mustn't go chasing after every tiny little wisp of smoke you see."

"Only big ones you mean?" said the witch.

"Of course," said the Chief Fire Officer.

"Then there's a very big one over there."

At first, no one bothered to look, until the witch took the cricket stumps away and pointed, "Over *there!*"

"Oh my golly!" gasped Harry. "Now that's

what I call a big un!"

"You noticed me noticin' it didn't you?" said the witch.

But the firemen were struggling into their boots and things.

It was Bill's job to drive, but the witch wanted another turn.

"Blimey!" said Bill. "I think the school's on fire!"

It was. Or rather, the school hall was blazing away. Smoke as black as night was pouring out of the windows and there was an orange light glowing brightly in the open doorway. The witch forgot to think how super it looked because she was worried about Simon. Simon was her best friend and she didn't want him to get hurt. But the children had had fire drill thousands of times and they were all standing in tidy lines in the playground.

"We're missing arithmetic," grinned Simon.

"Multiplication of decimals!" added Jimmy Watson, astonished at his good luck.

"Missing important lessons is not funny," scoffed Sally.

"Everybody else is laughing," said the witch, squirting quite a lot of water on Sally, by mistake on purpose.

Bill and Harry were starting to put out the fire

in the hall when the witch asked, "Has anyone taken the register?"

"Taken it where Sir, I mean Madam?" grinned Jimmy Watson, nervously.

"Don't be a silly little boy," said the witch. "I mean – called out the names to see if everyone is here and saved."

"Mr Bodley isn't here," yawned Sally. "He usually takes the register."

"Isn't here? Then where is he?"

"Counting the dinner money I expect," yawned Sally again.

"You mean he'd rather be burnt to death and turned into a little gritty black cinder than lose his dinner money?" said the witch.

"Probably," said the children.

"He's bonkers!" said the witch.

"Yes," agreed the children, happily watching Harry and Bill and thinking that the arithmetic lesson was over and they should have been halfway through horrid History and now would never know how many wives Henry the Eighth had had.

"Poor old headmaster," grinned the witch. "I shall have to save the foolish greedy man. I shall have to force myself to be a heroine. I shall have to risk life and limb and me best black hat."

"Don't be silly," said Sally. "That part of the

school is not on fire."

The witch gave Sally a burning look and charged across the playground to fetch a ladder. The children stopped watching Bill and Harry and started to watch the witch, as she tucked her skirt into her baggy black knickers and began to climb the ladder.

Mr Bodley was still counting the dinner money when the witch cocked her leg over the window-sill and landed in a large heap on the floor.

"The school's on fire, Did you know?" she said.

"Fifteen, sixteen, seventeen," said Mr Bodley.

"The school hall's on fire. The Lady Fox-Custard hall."

"Eighteen, nineteen, twenty," said Mr Bodley.

"The hall the vicar paid for out of the bingo money."

"Twenty-one, twenty-two, twenty-three," counted the Head.

"The one the mayor opened."

"Twenty-four, twenty-five . . . *what*!?" gasped Mr Bodley, dropping a penny under the table. "Did you say the school hall was on fire?"

"Gosh!" sighed the witch. "It must be awful to be deaf when the whole school is burning down around you. Can't you smell it?"

"I thought it was just the smell of the school

dinners!" gasped Mr Bodley.

"Not unless you were having toad-in-the-hall!" sniggered the witch. "Did you notice me making that good joke?"

"No," said Mr Bodley, fainting because he'd have to give back all the dinner money to the children.

It was time for the witch to practise her firewoman's lift. She grabbed Mr Bodley behind the knees and yanked him down the ladder like a sack of potatoes.

"Did you notice me being a heroine?" she asked the children.

"Yes!" they said.

"Good," grinned the witch. "Next lesson's swimming."

"We haven't a swimming pool," scoffed Sally.

"Didn't have, you mean," said the witch.

Harry and Bill had squirted so much water into the school hall it was deep enough to swim in. The children cheered like anything.

"D'you think everyone's noticing me now?" the witch asked Simon, as she floated along on her back.

"Yes, I'm sure they are," laughed Simon.

"About time too!" spouted the witch, "I've had to go through fire and water to make them!" And she disappeared out of sight like a gigantic black whale.

The Jumble Sale

Mr Bodley, the Head, was very upset when he saw what was left of his lovely school hall. The children could swim in it only for a short time because Sally had spitefully opened the remains of the door and all the water had rushed out. And everybody had floated out with it and landed in the rose bushes. All that remained inside were a few rows of charcoal chairs, a soggy pile of black curtains, a few planks of the stage, and a picture of the mayor with a burnt nose. Where were the children going to do the school pantomime, or play games, or stand in lines to listen to him giving one of his interesting talks? And worst of all, where was the stage on which he, along with the vicar and the mayor and Lady Fox-Custard had so often sat, looking down on the parents at prize giving?

"You could have a raffle?" suggested Miss Phoeble, feebly.

"I had just thought of that," lied Mr Bodley. And he rummaged around his study, searching for something he didn't want. He came across a book called "1001 Things Every Child Should Know". It had been hidden away in a cupboard so long it didn't even mention the invention of the steam engine, but it had never been opened, and when Mr Bodley had squirted it with a bit of polish it looked slightly better.

He took the book around the classrooms and showed it to everyone, and everyone looked at it – gloomily.

"Of course, I'm not going to *force* anybody to buy a raffle ticket," said Mr Bodley, sternly, "but to know a thousand and one things would be a wonderful thing indeed."

Jimmy Watson thought that if he had to learn about a thousand and one things, his brain would surely explode and he'd drop down dead which wouldn't be so jolly wonderful, but he bought a ticket and hoped he wouldn't win. For a change, he felt glad that he was usually such an unlucky boy.

A few other children nervously bought tickets, and then Mr Bodley drew the winning number out of a hat. A boy called Smithy who was in the first form won the prize. On a good day, Smithy could just about manage to write his own name but that was all, and he stared at the book in utter horror. At playtime he swopped it with Sally for a piece of chewing gum.

Mr Bodley counted his winnings, but they only came to one pound and four pence. He was cross.

"Not even enough to pay a cleaning lady to brush up the floor," he complained to the teachers.

Then he remembered Lady Fox-Custard.

Lady Fox-Custard was very good at raising money. When she had one of her garden fêtes, or bring and buy sales, or coffee mornings, everyone went, because they wanted to look around her Ladyship's garden and peer through the windows of her very grand house. And everybody wanted to talk to her so that they could go home and say, "As I was talking to her Ladyship the other day. . ." and things like that.

And Lady Fox-Custard adored it too, because she could wear one of her extraordinary, floaty, garden fête dresses and drift around in it, looking so much posher than anyone else.

"I'd love to help you, headmaster," she treacled down the phone.

And she started to drive around the town at

once, ordering the mothers to make cakes, and knit bootees, and stuff darling little toys.

She knocked at the witch's door and the witch said, "I'm sorry, Mrs Custard, but I need all the stuff what I've got, because I'm having a jumble sale."

"A *jumble* sale!?" boomed Lady Fox-Custard. "Whatever for?"

"To get money to mend the school hall," said the witch, putting on a very simple face.

"But I'm doing that," said Lady Fox-Custard

The witch then put on a very astonished face and said, "Oh, well, you do yours and I'll do mine," and she shut the door.

44

At first, Lady Fox-Custard was furious, but then she laughed to herself and thought, "It will be some jumble sale! Wretched woman! And how does she think she's going to fit more than two and a half people into her scooty little garden?"

And so the days went by, and the mothers baked cakes, and clicked their knitting needles, and wearily stuffed darling little toys.

But Simon was cross with his mother. "Can't you bake those cakes for my friend's jumble sale?" he asked.

"Which friend is that, dear?" she asked.

"The witch," said Simon.

"Darling," said Simon's mother. "How many times have I told you not to call that unfortunate old woman a witch?"

And she went on baking cakes for the garden fête. Not because she wanted to, but simply because she was never any good at saying "No" to her Ladyship.

Meanwhile, the witch was making cunning plans to make her jumble sale a hundred thousand times better than Lady Fox-Custard's garden fête. She started collecting things from around her own house first and piled them on the kitchen table.

She found fifty pairs of black woolly stockings with only one small hole in each of the toes; a star with a point broken off it; some tins of cat food which were too good to be wasted on George; some books on magic which had gone out of date; and, at the back of a cupboard, a superb stuffed crocodile her sister, Tombola, had sent her from Africa, and had the blessed advantage of not needing feeding or taking for walks. The crocodile, the witch decided, was far too good just to go on a stall, so she would raffle it.

Next day, she called on the mothers, just as Lady Fox-Custard had done. But the mothers looked at the witch without much interest and said that they'd given all their things to the garden fête and couldn't be bothered to make anything else.

The witch was quietly furious, but smiled in a jolly sort of way and said, "Not to worry, mumsies, I'm sure the dear little kiddiewinkies will help a poor old woman to collect stuff for a jumble sale which is, after all, to raise money for a new school hall and not to build a new wing on her own humble abode."

At this, some of the mothers looked a little bit guilty, but they still couldn't be bothered to make any more.

"I fink that's a shame!" said Smithy. He pulled his shirt out of his trousers and polished his glasses. "I fink if we all tidied our cupboards and fings, we could find a fousand and one fings we don't want." (He was mostly thinking of horrid reading books he couldn't read).

"Hear! Hear!" said Jimmy Watson.

"I agree," said Simon.

"You've all gone soft in the head – helping that old crone!" scoffed Sally. But she secretly agreed that a jumble sale sounded much more fun than a garden fête. All the children hated Lady Fox-Custard's fêtes. They were quite unbelievably boring. Not only that, Lady Fox-Custard over-charged for everything. She cut small cakes in half, watered the lemonade; and her ice-creams were almost invisible. To make things worse, she made her gardener go round bellowing at everyone to keep off the grass, and as most of her garden was grass she seemed to expect the children to walk upside down on the sky.

So the children suddenly got very interested in the witch's jumble sale and started to collect a lot of things.

"It's great isn't it!" beamed Simon, as he helped the witch to pile up the stuff on the kitchen table.

"No more than I expected," lied the witch, smiling craftily at a book called "1001 Things Every Child Should Know."

"Oh, that book's out of date," said Simon.

"I was thinking it would make a better raffle prize than the stuffed crocodile."

"No," said Simon. "It's *awful*."

But the witch took the book to bed with her, and when she'd finished laughing at it, she did something she didn't do a lot: she took out her magic wand and changed all the words and all the pictures until the book was so modern it explained things which hadn't even been invented yet.

The garden fête Saturday arrived and it was time for the witch to set out her jumble stalls. As there was no room in her garden, and she'd put up a 'Keep off the nasturtiums' sign anyway, she moved the tables out onto the pavement.

"Not on a public 'ighway you don't, Missus," said a policeman at once.

"You're having me on!" said the witch, astonished at this new navy blue problem in silver buttons.

"No I aren't," said the policeman, rocking importantly on his heels.

"Oh dear," thought the witch, not liking to wear out her magic wand twice in one week but having to change the policeman straightaway into a black beetle. The black beetle fell off the edge of the pavement into the gutter and struggled on his back. He was now so difficult to argue with, being about a thousandth of his original size – or maybe a millionth, the witch had to get down on her knees.

"I *need* the pavement!" she hissed. "There ain't no room in me garden. I've got a thousand and one things to sell."

The beetle tried to blow its whistle but couldn't manage.

"And when I change you back again . . . if I do, I want police cones all across the road. I don't want ten ton trucks grinding up it."

The beetle wished that his girl friend, Tilly, the most terrifically terriblest traffic warden wasn't on holiday in Blackpool. He wished that just with one of his legs he could dial 999, but he didn't think his chief would take much notice of a beetle, so he nodded his head frantically and was changed back to his proper size. Hastily, he put up NO ENTRY signs at the end of the road, and the witch finished her preparations.

Meanwhile, Lady Fox-Custard was opening her garden fête. She was wearing a long white floaty dress covered in poppies and her small mean mouth was painted like a poppy. Even her eyes were popping with satisfaction, when the mayor rolled up in his Rolls Royce, followed by the vicar, wobbling up the drive on his solid British bicycle, and then Mr Bodley in an old mini, its exhaust pipe popping like a machine gun.

"How lovely to see you!" she gushed, giving them all ice-creams, which were so small they were almost not worth bothering about.

Simon's mother had made such lovely big fairy cakes her ladyship had ordered the gardener to cut them in halves, but was careful not to cut the price tickets in half.

"Oh gosh!" wailed Jimmy Watson, who had had his pocket money halved for leaving the bathroom light on all night, "I can't hardly afford nothing!"

"There's a better sale on down the road," reminded Simon.

At once, all Simon's friends wanted to go to the better sale. Even Sally, who was stuck up, but nevertheless didn't like being diddled, followed Simon down to the witch's house.

What a jumble of exciting things met their eyes! There were old model trains, piles of comics, antique dolls, water pistols, secondhand fireworks, and of course – the raffle for the book, "1001 Things Every Child Should Know." The policeman, who had been changed into a beetle and back again, was very anxious to keep in the witch's good books and was busy re-directing the traffic. Every time a number twenty-five bus came round the corner, he made everybody get off and buy a raffle ticket.

George was sitting on a swing over a bucket of water and there was a sign above him saying,

DROWN THE CAT AND WIN 10p

Simon thought this was a bit cruel until he noticed that George had stuck his tail to the swing with a strip of sticky tape. For 2p. the children could watch the witch do a daring parachute jump. All she actually did was to climb onto her garden wall, put up her umbrella and leap into the nasturtiums.

"What a swizz!" said Sally.

But the other children thought it was terribly funny.

As the witch jumped and showed off, parents began to arrive to collect their children. And as it so happened, the mayor, the vicar and the headmaster all got re-directed by the policeman who was still dead keen on not being turned back into a beetle.

"I say! What fun!" beamed the mayor when he saw all the pavement stalls and lemonade at only a penny a glass.

"Awfully jolly," agreed the vicar.

"Maybe. Maybe not!" grunted Mr Bodley.

"Ah! Your battleship!" greeted the witch.

"Worship!" hissed Simon.

"Warship," said the witch. "You're just in time to draw the winning raffle ticket."

"A pleasure," boomed the mayor.

And Smithy won the book "1001 Things Every Child Should Know" back again.

At first, his face crumpled up, but when he saw how many new pictures the witch had magicked into it, he was really pleased.

But the best part came when Mr Bodley added up all the money. Lady Fox-Custard had raised fifty pounds and the witch had raised fifty pounds and one pence. Lady Fox-Custard was livid. The witch gave one of her infuriating toothy grins and Mr Bodley, the headmaster, was forced to thank the witch very much for her noble effort.

"It was nothing, your-know-all-ship," said the witch.

And so the burnt school hall was redecorated and everything.

The Battle of Hastings

With a new school hall, Mr Bodley seemed to go around looking all new himself. He threw away his Oxfam jacket and bought himself a smart, new, navy blazer with brass buttons all over it. He stood on the stage, arms behind his back, beamed at the sea of faces below him, and said, "I've got a wonderful surprise for you children, we're going to go on a day trip to Boulogne. How's that!?"

"Ooooh," said the children, wondering if it meant more tents and stampeding cows.

"Boulogne is a fishing town in France. We will take the ferry from Dover and cross the English Channel."

The children began to look suddenly interested, and astonished.

"Of course," went on Mr Bodley, intelligently, "in France, everybody speaks French so I shall be teaching you a few useful phrases."

"Oh no!" groaned Jimmy Watson. "I knew there'd be a catch in it somewhere."

"I did too," agreed Simon.

"You lot are lazy and stupid!" scoffed Sally. "I look upon this as a great educational opportunity."

The rest of the class gawped at Sally dumbly.

After tea, Simon dashed round to see the witch.

"Guess what!" he puffed.

"You're going on a day trip to Boulogne."

"How did you know?" gasped Simon.

"I didn't. You told me to guess," said the witch. "Anyway, I think two holidays in one year is shocking, but seeing as how it couldn't possibly be worse than the camping one I might as well come on it."

"Oh, but I'm afraid you can't," said Simon, looking embarrassed. "Mr Bodley said no one will be allowed to come if they don't learn French."

"*That's* no problem," grinned the witch, popping a crusty spider into her soup and drinking it. "I learnt myself French *years* ago."

"Oh good," said Simon, pleased that his friend would be coming on the trip, but vaguely worried at the same time.

As soon as he had gone, the witch grabbed her Book of Magic Spells which contained answers to absolutely everything and feverishly started to hunt through the 'Fs' to find French. There was F for Fat, F for Fabulous Fruit Fudge, F for Furry Frog, and at last, F for French. There were four hundred and forty-four pages, but the witch, who had had hundreds of years' practice in learning magic spells by heart, taught herself French in five minutes and went to bed, booming at her cat, "Bon nuit, mon chat." George, who yet again had had no supper, wasn't in the mood for a chat so he ignored the remark.

Meanwhile, Mr Bodley was vastly enjoying being a French master. Clutching a book he'd had since he was a boy, he collected the children around him.

"This is the pen of my aunt," he said in French.

"This is the pen of my aunt," droned the children.

"My grandmother is wearing a green dress."

"My grandmother is wearing a green dress."

"In Jean Pierre's garden are two goldfish," Mr Bodley went on.

The children began to yawn.

"Jimmy Watson!" barked Mr Bodley. "If you're not going to try you're not coming."

"But Sir," complained Jimmy, "we haven't got no goldfish in our garden. Only beans and things."

Mr Bodley sighed and went on, "I am wearing a big hat."

"I am wearing a big hat," repeated the children.

The day at last arrived for them to set off for Dover, and there, waiting for them by the ferry stood the witch. She was wearing a large pair of dark sunglasses and a black beret.

"I don't believe it!" groaned Mr Bodley.

Miss Phoeble trembled.

The witch produced an innocent smile which oddly did not suit her.

"You'll be telling me next you speak fluent French!" snapped Mr Bodley.

"Certainement," agreed the witch, and led the way onto the ferry.

All the way across the Channel, the witch behaved angelically and Miss Phoeble stopped trembling. But Simon, who sat next to the witch, had the feeling he was sharing a seat with an unexploded bomb.

The unexploded bomb disembarked with the rest of the school and marched along the side of the harbour wall. A group of fishermen in blue overalls and brown wellingtons glanced at the witch curiously and she glanced at them. On towards a café, Mr Bodley led the troupe. Jimmy Watson was dismayed to see that the menu was all in French.

"That's because we happen to be in France!" scoffed Sally.

But the witch snapped her fingers at the waiter and ordered Frites et Poissons for the children, which, to their delight, turned out to be fish and chips. Mr Bodley couldn't understand one word on the menu but was determined not to order the same as the witch, so he asked for escargots.

"*Snails*, them are," whispered the witch to Simon, gleefully.

When they arrived, Miss Phoeble screamed loudly and fled, whilst Mr Bodley, accidently on purpose, dropped his plate on the floor.

Some of the snails seemed to have come alive and slithered away huffily.

Outside on the pavement, Mr Bodley pulled himself together with an effort and said that they were going to visit the cathedral – La Basilique Notre Dame.

He was not sure of the way, so he stopped an old woman who was wearing a black shawl round her head and looked as if she might be going to church herself. But the old woman looked puzzled and shook her head.

"Probably she doesn't want to know about the pen of his aunt and all that stuff!" sniggered Jimmy Watson behind his hand.

"I'll deal with this," said the witch, trotting up to the old woman and speaking to her in hundred-mile-an-hour French and throwing her arms about a lot.

"Ah oui! Oui! Oui!" nodded the aged woman, also throwing her arms about a lot and pointing up the hill.

Peevishly, Mr Bodley led the way, snapping, "Walk properly you lot, I don't want people thinking St. Wilfred's is a school for young hooligans."

When they at last arrived, puffing and bored, Mr Bodley said, "Stay where you are and wait," and he disappeared inside a shop with Miss Phoeble to buy postcards.

Everyone gazed up at the large grey cathedral which to them looked the same as any other, give or take a stone squiggle here and there.

"Right!" said the witch, "I guess we've seen it now. The inside'll be pretty much the same as the outside. Let's go."

"But we can't!" gasped Jimmy Watson, aghast.

"We can if we run," said the witch. And grabbing up her skirts she started to race back down the hill like a bat in full flight.

The children raced after her and forgot about the terrible trouble they would probably get into later when they were found.

Now, Boulogne seemed a really exciting place, especially when they came to the crowded side streets and the foreign looking shops and people talking in real French everywhere. Simon bought his mother some sugared almonds, tied up in a little muslin bag. And Smithy bought himself a tin ladybird with red spots on it.

"Oh look!" cried Sally in delight, "pink wooden clogs! I'll look great in those at the disco."

"Especially if you wear a pillow case over your

head," said the witch, who didn't like Sally a lot.

Down the next street was a bakery and the children couldn't believe their eyes when they saw the loaves of bread.

"They're about a mile long!" gasped Jimmy Watson, exaggerating slightly.

Everyone wanted one, and they had just about enough money left to buy a loaf each.

"The smell's making me hungry," groaned Simon. "I'll never get mine home in one piece."

"That reminds me!" exclaimed the witch. "My cat hasn't been fed."

For the first time, the children noticed a scruffy black ear sticking out of the corner of the witch's handbag.

"You've *never* brought George have you?" gasped Simon.

"Why not?" said the witch. "A cat can have a holiday can't it?"

She hadn't forgotten the fishermen down by the harbour which she remembered was near a street called La Grande Rue.

The same group of fishermen was still sitting on the wall, still smoking, and slurping out of a bottle of brandy. They had just returned with a boatful of herring and were waiting to have them weighed in and refrigerated. Interested to see the witch again, they agreed they had plenty of fish to spare for one small cat and invited everyone aboard.

"What a stink!" complained Sally, slithering about on the deck.

The witch was making herself instantly at home, sitting on the deck and chatting to the fishermen about the dangerous sea voyages she herself had managed single handed, and smoking black cigarettes which she kept craftily getting rid of by tossing them overboard. George was munching his way through his forty-fifth fish and spitting bones everywhere, whilst the children sunbathed and thought how much more fun this was than having to trail round a cathedral with Mr Bodley and Miss Phoeble, each agreeing

how marvellous each separate stone was.

"Another brandy, Madame?" one of the fishermen was asking the witch, when a nearby clock suddenly struck six.

"Gosh!" said the witch, wobbling somewhat. "Our ferry sails in ten minutes!" And kissing all the fishermen on both cheeks, she grabbed the children and charged them along to the landing stage.

Mr Bodley was purple with fury, but oddly speechless, and Miss Phoeble stood there shaking like an un-set raspberry jelly.

"When you vanished, headmaster," said the witch, slyly, "I was very worried, but luckily I was able to show the children round Boulogne myself."

Mr Bodley went on being speechless.

When the ferry was under way, Jimmy Watson said, "Can we go up on the top deck, Sir? It's boring down here."

"You can go where you like," muttered Mr Bodley.

The top deck was already crowded and there was nowhere to sit. Also, the ferry was rolling somewhat so that Smithy's loaf of bread struck Jimmy Watson across the neck.

"You hit me with that, you great elephant!" yelled Jimmy, and held up his own loaf of bread like a sword.

"That's it!" squealed the witch, "we'll have a battle! Think of a battle we could play."

"The Battle of Hastings," obliged Sally. "In 1066 the French crossed the Channel to fight the English."

"That'll do," said the witch. "And who was their leader?" she wanted to know.

"William The Conqueror."

"Right, I'll be him then," said the witch, looking round craftily at the children from other schools who could play the enemy.

"No," objected Simon. "We can't attack *them*. They're unarmed."

"O.K." agreed the witch. "We'll just have to fight each other."

Delighted, the children crossed bread loaves and a fierce battle began. As lumps of bread flew everywhere, a crowd of screeching seagulls gathered and swooped down.

"Great!" panted the witch. "The airforce is coming to help our side."

"They didn't have aeroplanes in 1066!" snorted Sally.

The witch swiped the top off Sally's bread which meant she was as good as dead. The seagulls were enjoying the battle as much as the children and dive-bombed at the pieces of falling bread before they had time to hit the deck. Groups of peace-loving pensioners began to complain loudly which, to the witch, made the glorious battle even more exciting – but not in the opinion of the second officer. He boomed over the public address system, "Would the headmaster in charge of St. Wilfred's kindly come up and control his group."

"Hah! A new enemy!" shrieked the witch, charging with what was left of her bread sword, a crazed seagull clinging giddily to her hat.

The second officer decided not to bother about being a hero and beat a hasty retreat to the safety of the bridge. Moments later he bellowed, "Point alpha!" which meant it was nearly time to land.

As they piled off the ferry at Dover, Mr Bodley

bawled, "Don't imagine I'm ever going to take you on holiday again. Just don't even imagine it."

Battle-scarred, but happy, the children followed him through Customs.

"Nothing to declare!" he snapped, pushing them all through the green barrier.

"You'll get into trouble if you don't declare that cat," Simon whispered to the witch. "There's a rabies law — he'll have to go into quarantine."

The witch hadn't the faintest idea what Simon was going on about but hastily fumbled around with her handbag.

There was something about the witch's extraordinarily innocent expression which aroused the suspicion of one of the customs men.

"What have you got in that handbag, Madame?" he asked.

"Nothing," said the witch.

"Nothing?"

"I tell a lie," said the witch, "I've got some French fresh air. Thought it would be good for my garden."

"Don't you get smart with me, old woman," said the customs man, and grabbed the handbag.

To Sally's disappointment, it was empty.

"I find that very odd," the customs man went

on, "a lady with an empty handbag!"

"I'm dead poor," sighed the witch.

"I wonder what would happen if I were to get hold of you by the ankles and shake you upside down?" threatened the customs man.

"You'd probably get arrested," said the witch.

But at that moment, George, whose claws were getting weak hanging on to the witch's knickers, let go and fell to the ground.

"Great fool!" the witch barked at him.

"Hah! I thought there was something fishy about *you*!" the customs man looked pleased with himself.

"Wrong again," shrugged the witch. "It's him what's fishy."

George was covered in flakes of herring scales; he had a half eaten fish stuck behind his ear and the remains of a fish's tail hanging out of his mouth.

"Disgusting animal!" said Sally.

The customs man rattled on. "Of course you know it's against the law to bring an animal into the country. I shall have to confiscate that . . . cat and keep it in quarantine for six months."

The witch shrugged again. It would be quite peaceful doing without George for a few months.

"You can keep 'im in any kind of quarry m'jig you like," she said, and trotted off with the others towards the coach.

The last thing she saw was the customs man, gingerly trying to scoop George up with a shove'

"That cat's on a special diet," she yelled over her shoulder. "He only eats furniture."

The Cure for George

Not long after George was returned to the witch he fell ill. When she came down for breakfast one morning she found him on the kitchen floor. He was lying on his back with his four legs sticking up stiffly into the air.

"Get up, you fool!" said the witch (she had a way with animals).

But George stayed where he was and stared glassily at the ceiling.

The witch wasn't in the mood for playing doctors and nurses so early in the morning, so she ignored him and sat down to a breakfast of cornflakes and crushed crab shells.

An hour later, Simon arrived. "What's wrong with your cat?" he asked.

"Dunno," munched the witch. "I think he's

just playing one of his games."

"He looks dead to me," Simon said, worried about George's stiff posture.

"Of course he's not," scoffed the witch. "The fur on his tummy's going up and down. He can't be dead if his fur's going up and down."

The witch's cat was always doing strange things so Simon went home. But when he returned next day, George was still on the kitchen floor with his legs in the air.

"I really do think that cat's ill," said Simon. "It's not normal for an animal to stay like that for so long."

"It's not convenient either," said the witch. "If he doesn't behave himself soon, I'll step on him."

"I think you should take him to the vet," Simon said.

"That's a rotten idea," humphed the witch. "Vets charge money."

"But if you don't he might die, and then you'll have no cat."

The witch looked solemn at that. Her wretched relation, Sarah Screech, had two cats. It was bad enough to own only one cat — if she was left with none at all she'd be disgraced as a witch.

"All right," she said, and, lifting George up by his paws, she stumped off to the vet.

There was a long queue, which didn't make the witch feel any jollier. At the head of the queue was a goldfish with fungus on its fin. Then came a guinea pig with a bandage round its head. Next to it was a rabbit with a streaming cold, sneezing germs onto everybody else. And next to the inconsiderate rabbit was a boy with a jar of tadpoles. On a good day, George would have enjoyed annoying the lot of them. But he did nothing. The witch wanted to go first but no one would let her.

"Don't you know what a queue is?" scolded the lady with the mouldy goldfish.

"Of course I do. It's the letter which comes before *you*!" snapped the witch.

"Right," said the snooty lady, "so 'u' comes after the 'q'."

"That's bad grammar," argued the witch.

When it was at last her turn to go into the surgery, she plonked George onto the table.

"Not like that," said the vet.

"That's the way he's been all week."

"What's the matter with him?"

"If I knew that," said the witch, "I wouldn't be wasting time and money bringing him here. He's trying to fool me he's ill."

"He does look a little pale I must say," said the vet.

"That's daft," said the witch. "How can he look pale when he's as black as ink?"

The vet ignored that and started to examine George carefully.

"Is he always as stiff as this?" he asked, as the cat continued to lie on its back with its legs stuck up in the air like four black bottle brushes.

The witch was getting tired of the vet's silly questions and decided to go home. She took the bottle of medicine he gave her but refused to pay him more than 5p for it because she said that all he'd told her was that George shouldn't be lying on his back all the time and she already knew that.

She measured the medicine on to a spoon and poured it into George's mouth. But as George's teeth were tightly shut, the medicine trickled along his whiskers and round the back of his neck.

"Ungrateful animal!" shrieked the witch, storming off to bingo.

When Simon came to visit her a week later, George was still in the same position on the kitchen floor.

"That's awful!" Simon said.

"I know," grumbled the witch. "I have to mop round him."

"I don't just mean that, I mean it's awful to go on taking no notice. He might die."

The witch had been secretly worrying about that too. How daft she'd look amongst her relations — a witch with no cat.

"All right," she muttered, "I'll write to my sister, Tombola."

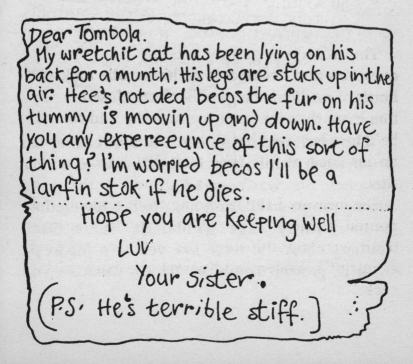

Dear Tombola.
My wretchit cat has been lying on his back for a munth. His legs are stuck up in the air. Hee's not ded becos the fur on his tummy is moovin up and down. Have you any expereeunce of this sort of thing? I'm worried becos I'll be a larfin stok if he dies.
      Hope you are keeping well
            LUV
                  Your sister.
(P.S. He's terrible stiff.)

And she posted it to Jungle Grove, Africa.
Tombola replied at once.

SISTER,
DEAR HEART
I KNOW EXACTLY WHATS WRONG
WITH YOUR CAT— HE'S <u>BORED</u> STIFF.
I ONCE HAD A GORILLA WITH THE
SAME COMPLAINT. THINK YOURSELF
LUCKY GEORGE IS ONLY A SKINNY WEE
BEAST. THIS GORILLA I'M TELLING YOU
ABOUT DECIDED TO GET BORED STIFF IN MY
LIVING ROOM. I HAD TO SIT OUTSIDE MY HOUSE
FOR A WHOLE YEAR AND WATCH TELLY
THROUGH THE WINDOW. IF THE WEATHER
FORECAST IS GOOD, I MIGHT COME AND SEE
YOU. —KIND REFARDS— TOMBOLA.
P.S. MY POT'S BOILING OVER. SNAKES ARE
WRITHING EVERYWHERE.

The witch had no sooner finished reading the
letter when Tombola arrived with a thud on her
doorstep. She was covered all over with a very
strong jungle smell, and next to her towered an
extraordinarily large gorilla. He had a black
leathery chest and teeth like yellow piano keys.

"Hi!" greeted Tombola. "This is Banana – you

know, the bored gorilla I was telling you about. Cured. Full of fun now."

Banana bombed across the kitchen, opened the witch's tin of beetles and ate them in one loud crunch with his piano key teeth.

"Full of fun!" repeated Tombola.

"And beetles," remarked the witch.

For once, she didn't quite know what to do, except to get Banana out of her house, because whoever had built her house hadn't measured it up to include gorillas.

"Maybe we could go for a stroll," she suggested.

"Good idea," beamed Tombola. "It's stuffy in here."

They wandered off down the road, the witch carrying George under her arm, and Banana, rolling along the pavement like a demented hearthrug out on a day trip. Round the corner was the school where the children were just lining up in the playground to go indoors.

Banana peered through the railings in astonishment. He had never seen so many chimpanzees in one bunch. Pink, hairless chimpanzees – dressed up in funny clothes. He loped up the railings and swung himself into their midst.

"A *gorilla*!" screamed Jimmy Watson in delighted terror.

"Silence!" squeaked Miss Phoeble, who had her back to Banana.

"Wouldn't you know!" snorted Sally. "It's that witch woman again with some of her relations."

"Hurry along children," Miss Phoeble was saying, unnecessarily for a change, as the children stampeded into the school. Grinning hugely, Banana raced after them. This was enormous fun, he thought, as he watched the children running down the corridor and scattering into different rooms. He decided to leap into Simon's classroom, followed hotly by Tombola and the witch, still clasping George the cat.

"Oh gosh!" gasped Simon, as the gorilla pushed him out of the way and sat in his place. "What's going on?"

"Search me!" said the witch. "It's all to do with the treatment my sister's giving George. Says he's stiff 'cos he's bored – like her gorilla used to be. Ordinary common complaint, she said."

"I *will* not have all this noise!" Miss Phoeble squeaked again, opening the register.

Then she saw the gorilla in Simon's place, and promptly fainted.

Banana shot across the floor, scooped her up under his arm and jumped with her onto the top of the Art cupboard, where he sat, shaking Miss Phoeble and thumping his leathery chest and wondering why the little old teacher didn't want to play with him.

"Naughty Banana!" scolded Tombola. "Put that lady down at once." The gorilla did so, and the amazed children watched their form mistress fall like a stone from the top of the Art cupboard.

"It's lucky for you she landed on the bean bags," Sally shouted at Tombola.

"It's lucky for her too," said Tombola. "My gorilla may be a bit careless but he's not a vandal you know."

Banana seemed to disprove this last remark by wrenching the lid off Simon's desk and using it as a cricket bat. Then he tore up Simon's homework into hundreds of little pieces and threw it over himself to pretend he'd just got married. The children couldn't believe it. They had given up being terrified of Banana and had begun to laugh at him – all except for Sally, who thought the gorilla's behaviour was shocking. Banana liked being laughed at and began to scribble on the blackboard. Meanwhile, Sally decided things had gone far enough and went to fetch the Head.

Mr Bodley thought Sally must be sickening for something – chattering on about there being a gorilla in the classroom, and came along to tell Miss Phoeble that Sally had better go home and have a lie down. But to his dismay, he found that there really *was* a gorilla in the classroom, and

two witches, and a cat, and Miss Phoeble, asleep on a pile of beanbags. He opened his mouth and shut it again several times. Banana thought that Mr Bodley must be dumb and felt very sorry for him, so he put his arms round the headmaster and hugged him, kindly. Mr Bodley didn't realize it was a kind hug and went pale purple in the face because he couldn't breathe.

"Put that gentleman down! Banana!" scolded Tombola again.

Banana was getting tired of making new friends and then being told to put them down again. He liked Mr Bodley very much and wanted to keep him so he hung on to him even more tightly.

All this time, the witch was sitting in the corner, enjoying herself hugely. Mr Bodley had given up struggling, but he felt ridiculous and in the wrong position for saying, "I am very displeased with this class," and that sort of thing.

The witch thought it was the funniest thing she had seen for ages. Of course, she had always known Mr Bodley was no good as a headmaster. He had absolutely no sense of humour. A properly trained headmaster would have known exactly what to do with a friendly gorilla. Banana knew what to do with Mr Bodley: he dropped him on the floor with a thud.

"Wow!" gasped Jimmy Watson, who was more used to looking up to his headmaster.

Feeling suddenly brave, the children started to do as they liked – which was drawing houses on the blackboard with coloured chalk.

Banana wanted to draw a house too, and so did the witch, when suddenly, Simon cried, "Look!"

The fur on George's tummy was beginning to twitch; his legs unstiffened, and he let out a long howling meiow.

"What's that ridiculous animal doing now?" snorted Sally.

"Getting better!" whooped the witch. "Deciding not to die of boredom. Making new friends."

She said this as George hurled himself across the room at Banana. Banana caught him like a rugby ball. He was delighted when he discovered that George wanted to play booma booma with him.

Booma booma was a game none of the children would have dared to play. It was jumping on and off desks. The noise woke up Miss Phoeble and brought Mr Bodley to his senses. He looked at his watch.

"Home time," he said.

"But it's only half past two," said Sally.

"I've got a staff meeting," Mr Bodley said. So everybody went.

"Will Banana be staying with you long?" Simon asked the witch on the way down the road.

"Not if I can help it!" said the witch, "the great . . . gorilla!"

"Yet he did cure your cat of boredom," Simon reminded her. "You should be grateful."

"I'd have a grate full all right if that oversized chimp stayed," snorted the witch, hurrying ahead to tell Tombola that the weather for flying was ideal.

Simon was shocked at the witch's outrageous behaviour, but then he laughed.

After all, she was an outrageous person. And his friend.